Tales from the BOX

Boolar's
Big Day Out

Sally Gardner

BLOOMSBURY
CHILDREN'S
BOOKS

Chapter One

Autumn and falling leaves came as a terrible shock to the five little dolls who had lived happily all summer long in a box in the park, the same box that had been left under a bush outside Mr and Mrs Mouse's house. You would hardly recognise it now that it has been turned into a comfortable home with proper windows and its own front door.

This is where the Countess, Boolar, Ting Tang and Quilt live. Stitch, the fifth little doll, had never got over his fear of Mr Cuddles, the park keeper's cat, and had decided to live with Mr and Mrs Mouse instead.

This arrangement suited
them all very well indeed.

The long hot summer had been a
glorious one. So steady had been the
pattern of warm balmy days that the
dolls quite believed this was the way it
would stay for ever. Then suddenly
something changed, not in the weather
but in their dear friends, Mr and Mrs
Mouse.

Gone were the long lazy days and the
jolly evenings. Gone were meals eaten
together outside under a canopy of
stars. Gone were other mice popping
round for a chat and a gossip. Now life
seemed to be nothing but hard work
and food gathering.

Mrs Mouse started to spend all
her time frantically cooking and

filling up an assortment of pots and jars with jams and fruit preserves. The Countess helped as much as she could, chopping and peeling, but it was hard to understand why Mrs Mouse was in such a state.

Mr Mouse was in a terrible tizzy too, busily making lists and saying, 'Oh, bother my whiskers, we are short of this, we are short of that,' and 'Oh dear me, will we ever have enough?'

For some time, the tricky business of food gathering had been left in the capable hands of Boolar and Quilt. They too were baffled as to what was going on. No sooner had they got back to Mr Mouse with a sack full of food, which would usually have kept them going for a week or more, than he flapped and flustered so much that they felt obliged to go straight out again and gather more.

Mrs Mouse insisted they took the old pram with them to carry the sacks. Even then, when they came back with the pram filled as high as could be, Mr Mouse would not greet them with his usual cry of, 'A feast, my dear friends, you have brought back a feast!' Instead, he would say to Mrs Mouse, 'Oh my ribbly rodent, oh, the love of my whiskers, what will become of us?' And then he would put on his jacket, take up an empty sack and threaten to go out himself.

At this, Ting Tang, the Countess and Stitch would all set to crying and beg him to stay.

'No, my love,' Mrs Mouse would cry, 'you can't! What would happen to all of us if Mr Cuddles caught you?'

One day Boolar had had enough.

'Stop it,' he shouted. He was quite exhausted with all this rushing around. 'What is going on? Will someone please tell me?'

Chapter 2

Mr and Mrs Mouse stopped what they
were doing and looked at Boolar and the
other dolls in astonishment.

'You mean you don't know?' said Mr
Mouse, putting down the list he was
holding. 'Oh, twitch my whiskers,
you must know.'

'But we don't,' said Quilt.

'It's the betwixt and between
time,' explained Mrs Mouse.

'Never heard of it,' said
the Countess flatly.

Mr Mouse took out a
large spotted hankie
and mopped his brow.

'It's when the wind
blows and the leaves

fall down,' he said. 'Then when the
trees are quite bare, and the betwixt
and between time has passed, Jack
Frost comes to the park and, being very
cold and hard, he keeps the legs away.'

'No,' said Ting Tang, 'the trees can't
lose their leaves. That would be silly.'

'I quite agree,' added the Countess.
'I never heard of such a thing in the
Land of Lounge.'

'Well, this is not the Land of Lounge.
This is the park. This is what happens
here,' said Mr Mouse.

'It does sound a bit pointless,' said
Quilt. 'Why go to all the bother of
having leaves in the first place if you
are just going to throw them away?'

'It all has a point,' said Mr Mouse,
looking confused, 'though what that

point is, I'm not sure. It's a mystery too mighty for the mind of a mere mouse.'

'Who's Jack Frost?' asked Stitch. 'Is he like Mr Cuddles?'

'No, my love,' said Mrs Mouse. 'He's invisible. They say he wears a long white coat and his breath makes things go white too. Sometimes, though not often, he brings snow to stay.'

The dolls looked at each other, still none the wiser.

'Some years,' said Mr Mouse, trying his best to explain, 'Jack Frost is kind and mild. In those times not all the legs go away and there is still food to be found, but other times he can be very cruel

indeed. It's all a matter of reading the signs.'

'I'm scared,' said Stitch, going to Mrs Mouse for a hug.

'What are the signs?' asked Quilt.

'If the bushes are full of berries that's one way we know it will be a cold winter,' said Mrs Mouse, her arm firmly round Stitch.

'There are other signs too but it's a mouse thing,' said Mr Mouse with pride. 'My whiskers tell me Mr Frost is going to be hard on us this year and, what with so many to feed, we need to have the wood for the fire piled high and our storeroom full to brimming. Then when Jack Frost comes, we can all be warm and snug indoors.'

Mr Mouse started rummaging on the table for his list. 'Oh, bother my whiskers, that reminds me,' he said. 'Beeswax. We must get beeswax.'

'This all sounds very unnecessary,' said the Countess. 'Why don't I go and talk to this Jack Frost chap and tell him to keep away. He's not wanted. He has no right to go around frightening you like this.'

Mrs Mouse chuckled. 'That's kind of you, my dear, but he's going to come, whatever we say or do.'

'In that case,' said Boolar, still feeling muddled, 'like Mr Mouse says, we must make sure that our wood is piled high and our storeroom is full to bursting before the end of the betwixt and between time.'

'You mustn't worry,' said Quilt, patting

Mr Mouse on the back. 'Boolar and I
will take care of everything. We are here
to help.'

Early that evening, after the legs had
left the park and the gates were closed,
Boolar and Quilt went out food gathering
once more. The trees were bathed in a
golden light and the air was warm.
Boolar looked up at the leaves. 'Quilt, can
you imagine how any of this can change?'

'No,' said Quilt simply.

Chapter 3

A few weeks later the leaves began to fall. It was as if the trees were undressing, showing off their spindly scarlet and golden petticoats.

'If all those leaves tumble down we will be drowned, that's for sure,' said Quilt, standing one fine October morning beneath a large chestnut tree.

Suddenly something hard and prickly hit him on the head. For one awful moment Quilt's eyes rolled, and he swayed unsteadily on his feet.

Boolar rushed over to him.
'Are you all right?' he asked.

Quilt looked at him out of
one eye and said in a shaky voice,
'Everything seems to be ship-shape.'

'Where do you think that came from?'
asked Boolar.

Quilt was in the middle of saying he
hadn't a clue when thump! another one
hit him hard on the head again. This
time he wobbled, then fell face down in
a pile of leaves.

Now it is well known that lying
down in a pile of leaves is not a good
idea for a doll at the best of times, and
this was not the best of times. The park
was full of legs large and small rushing
backwards and forwards shouting,
'Conkers!'

17

Boolar knew he had to keep Quilt safe until the legs had gone home. He carefully dragged his friend under a park chair out of sight and there they waited.

Boolar must have fallen asleep, for when he looked out from his hiding place, the park was quite empty and it was getting dark.

'Quilt, are you feeling better?' asked Boolar, looking at his friend's pale face.

Quilt mumbled something about shape, sea and ship.

'Can you stand up?' asked Boolar, doing his best to help his friend. Quilt stood unsteadily for a moment before flopping down again.

It was no good. Boolar looked longingly over the gravel path towards the bush where the pram was hidden. It seemed like an ocean away and Quilt was too heavy for Boolar to lift by himself.

Then, to Boolar's great relief, Natty Bargain came striding along the path. Natty was a badly-made frog, a soft toy who lived with a family of mice by the boating pond. He was not the most considerate of frogs but he would have to do.

'Natty,' called Boolar, 'over here! I need some help.'

'What's up, my old doll?' said Natty, walking across to Boolar with large springy steps. 'Hey,' he said, looking down at Quilt, 'sailor doll doesn't look too chirpy.'

'He's been hit on the head twice by something hard and prickly,' said Boolar, 'and I am trying to get him home.'

'Well, don't let me stop you,' said Natty, beginning to walk away. 'Places to go, dolls to meet!' he called as he waved a cheery goodbye.

'Come back,' shouted Boolar, 'can't you see I need your help?'

'Me?' said Natty, surprised. 'You want
me to help you? What do I get out of it?'

Boolar looked puzzled. 'Nothing,' he said.

Natty thought for a moment. 'Nope,'
he said, 'nothing doesn't do nothing
for me.' And he started to walk away
again, whistling.

Just in time, Boolar remembered
that the one thing that interested
Natty was food.

'All right,' said Boolar,
'what about a meal?'

Natty spun round, grinning. 'Why didn't you say so, my old doll?'

Boolar sighed as together he and Natty lifted Quilt into the pram. If only help had come in the shape of his good friend Mr Wolf instead of this greedy badly-made frog. But with the dark now beginning to creep in around them, and the leaves dancing in the breeze like shadowy ghosts, even help from a badly-made frog was better than no help at all.

Chapter 4

Mr Mouse was waiting
and worrying outside the
front door, a lantern in
his hand. 'Oh twitch my
whiskers,' he kept saying
over and over again. 'Oh twitch
my whiskers, where can they be?'

He wandered past the dolls' box to
the edge of the bush and, pushing back
the leaves, looked out into the dark
nothingness of the park.

Much to his relief, he heard whistling,
and then his name being called. In the
gloom he could just make out the shape
of Boolar, but there was no sign of
Quilt. Instead Natty Bargain rushed
up to him and dropped sacks

of food down on Mr
Mouse's slippers.
Then, without even a
'Hello' or 'Nice to
see you', Natty asked
eagerly, 'What's for
supper?' and hurriedly
disappeared inside, slamming
the front door behind him.

'I am so sorry,' said Boolar, leaning
on the pram, 'but I couldn't make it
home on my own.'

'That's all right, but where is Quilt?'
asked Mr Mouse, anxiously.

Boolar pointed sadly into the pram.
Mr Mouse lifted his lantern and saw
Quilt's pale face looking back at him.
He was mumbling shakily, 'Sea, ship
and shape.'

'Oh, twiddle my whiskers,'
said Mr Mouse, 'what happened?'

'We had a spot of trouble,' said Boolar,
as they lifted Quilt out of the pram and
opened the front door. 'Quilt got hit on the
head twice by something hard and prickly.'

'Oh dearie me,' said Mr Mouse.

They carefully placed the floppity
Quilt in a comfy chair near the fire
in the kitchen.

'You see, those trees throw down
more than leaves,' explained Boolar
as everyone gathered around Quilt.
Everyone, that is, except for Natty.
He was already sitting at the kitchen
table with knife and fork in hand and
a napkin tied round his neck.

The Countess looked shocked. 'Can't
you see that Quilt is unwell?' she said.

'That's nothing to do with me, my old
china,' said Natty. 'I just brought him
home. Job done, now, where's the grub?'

'Take no notice of him,'
said Boolar wearily.

'All he thinks about is food.'

'What else is there to think about?' asked Natty.

Mr Mouse fetched his medical bag and, putting it down on a small table, brought out bottles and bandages, oils and ointments. Then he carefully took off Quilt's hat to see what damage had been done.

'That's quite a nasty bang you have there,' said Mr Mouse, peering over his glasses at the bump on Quilt's head.

'Will he have to go to the puppet master to be mended?' asked Stitch worriedly, moving closer to have a better look.

'He will be all right, won't he?' said Ting Tang. 'I couldn't bear it if anything were to happen to Quilt.'

'This your first
betwixt and between
time then?' asked
Natty from the
kitchen table.
No one answered.
'The same thing
happened to me last
year,' he continued,
rocking noisily back and
forth in his chair. 'A conker knocked
me out cold and changed my good looks
for ever.'

Ting Tang turned round, took one look
at Natty and burst into tears.

Mrs Mouse put an arm round her. 'It
did no such thing, my dear,' she said.
'Take no notice of him.'

'Well, it did,' said Natty, 'so there.'

'You look the same now, Natty
Bargain,' said Mrs Mouse firmly, 'as
you did on the day you were found.'

'That's not true,' mumbled Natty.

Mr Mouse carefully bandaged Quilt's
head and gave him a teaspoon
of bright pink medicine.

'Well, we will have to see how
he is in the morning. Plenty of
rest, that's the ticket,' said Mr Mouse.
'Now let's get him to bed.'

Everyone helped, rushing around
making tea and filling up hot water
bottles. Everyone, that is, but Natty,
who continued to sit at the table and
bang his knife and fork on his plate.

In no time at all, Quilt was tucked up
in bed with soft feather pillows for his
head and a warm cup of Mrs Mouse's

special herb tea. It wasn't long before
he was fast asleep.

'I will stay with him,' said Ting Tang
to the others, 'in case he wakes up
and forgets where he is.'

'This is a pretty pickle and no
mistake,' said Mr Mouse quietly, when
they were all finally seated round the
kitchen table for supper. 'How is Boolar
going to manage to gather food all on
his own?'

Chapter 5

Now it is well known that a mouse feels
that it is his or her duty to look after
his or her guest, and give that guest
the very best a mouse has to offer.
Even if that guest happens to
be a very greedy and ungrateful frog.

That evening Natty Bargain ate all
the pie and he ate all the pudding. He
ate all the chocolates and drank most of
the elderflower wine and then said that
he wasn't going home until he had had
a good night's sleep.

When Natty had finally gone to bed,
gloom, like a heavy blanket on a warm
day, settled over the group of friends.
Everyone agreed that if Natty stayed
any longer he could and would eat the

storeroom bare.

'How,' asked Boolar, 'do Mr and Mrs Fickle cope with him?'

'The news from those parts isn't good,' said Mr Mouse, 'is it, my ribbly rodent?'

'No,' said Mrs Mouse. 'The Fickles don't think they have enough food to keep them going, not with so many children and a greedy frog to feed.'

'Well, they should just tell him to go,' said the Countess.

'It is not that easy,' said Mr Mouse. 'You see, having a doll as part of your family is thought to be very smart indeed. No mouse worth his whiskers would like it known that his doll was eating his family out of house and home. Other mice might say that Mr and Mrs Fickle weren't good providers, and that would never do.'

'Oh really, that's silly,' said the Countess. 'You would need an army of mice to keep that frog well stuffed. And in any case, he is not a doll, he is merely a soft toy.'

'Tomorrow,' said Boolar firmly, 'I will take Natty home.'

'Oh twiddle my whiskers,' said Mr Mouse, 'you can't just push a guest out. It's not the way a mouse should behave.'

'Fortunately,' said Boolar smiling kindly, 'I am not a mouse. And don't let's forget, we have a storeroom to fill.'

Chapter 6

The next day Quilt was feeling much better and this news cheered everyone up as they sat eating their breakfast. So busy were they talking about their plans for the day that they forgot about Natty until he sprang like a jack-in-the-box into the kitchen saying he was so hungry he could eat seventy sausages.

'Good morning to you,' said Boolar, 'there's fresh bread, jam, butter and hot chocolate to see you on your way.'

'That's not going to keep my night eyes shining,' said Natty, grabbing the whole loaf and spreading it with all the butter and jam on the table.

'I still want ss ...' he said, his mouth so full he could hardly speak, '... sausages.'

'Where are your manners?' asked the Countess angrily. 'That bread was meant for everyone.'

'Manners? Don't have 'em, don't want 'em,' said Natty through a shower of crumbs. 'I am a badly-made frog.'

Mr Mouse sighed and put on his coat.

'We should be getting along,' he said to Boolar.

Mrs Mouse looked worried. The Countess patted her hand and said, 'There's no need for Mr Mouse to go. I am perfectly capable of helping Boolar do the food gathering.'

'You!' laughed Natty. 'I would like to see you pushing the pram, my old china.'

'Don't you my old china me,' said the Countess angrily.

'It's all right,' interrupted Boolar. 'I have a helper for today.'

'Who?' everyone asked, amazed.

'Natty,' said Boolar, lifting the frog out of his chair. 'He is coming with me, and Mr Mouse is staying here and looking after Quilt.'

Natty started to struggle, saying that he wasn't obliged to go out food gathering. He was a guest and guests …

'Should be thrown out if they are greedy and ungrateful,' said the Countess, helping Boolar push Natty up the hall and out of the house.

It was late afternoon
and the pram was full
of food by the time
Boolar took a very
sulky Natty back
to his home by
the boating pond.

Mr and Mrs Fickle
lived under a statue of
a lady. At least, that was
where they used to live,
except for some reason
that Natty couldn't work
out, the front door had
vanished.

'It's gone,' he said.
'That's strange. It was
here yesterday and

the day before. In fact it has always been just here,' he said, scratching the top of his head.

'Odd, very odd,' said Boolar, walking slowly round the base of the statue, pushing back the bushes as he went, until he saw a front door almost hidden from view.

'That's pretty silly,' said Natty, 'to go moving front doors and making a frog feel all muddled.'

He pulled the bell. No one came. Boolar knocked on the door and still no one came, though whispering could be heard from inside.

'Don't open it,' someone squeaked. Then another voice added, 'If we are quiet, he might go away.'

'Anyone would think,' said Natty,

'that I am not wanted.'

'Perhaps,' suggested Boolar, 'if you want to be welcome, you should try helping Mr and Mrs Fickle instead of eating them out of house and home.'

'Help?' said Natty. 'Me, help? Look, my old doll, it's the mice who have to look after us, not the other way round.'

'But if you helped, maybe they wouldn't go moving the front door,' said Boolar.

Natty shrugged his shoulders and started banging on the door with his webbed hands until a thin pale-faced

mouse opened it a crack.

'Oh,' said Mrs Fickle sadly, 'you are back.'

'Oh course I am back, and I am very hungry,' said Natty, pushing his way inside.

'Oh dear,' said Mrs Fickle and then, seeing Boolar, she asked nervously, 'Do you want to come in too?'

'No,' said Boolar. 'Thank you but I should be getting home. I thought you might like this,' and he handed Mrs Fickle a sack of food.

'That's very kind of you, I'm sure,' she said, smiling weakly. 'Please send my best wishes to Mr and Mrs Mouse,' she added as she closed the door.

Boolar walked home, pushing the pram along the paths in the late afternoon sunlight. He was so lost in thinking that

no mouse should have to put up with
a guest like Natty that he didn't see the
piece of newspaper blowing in the breeze
until it had landed right on top of him.

This was one of the hazards of park life.
The legs left not only food behind them
but rubbish as well. Boolar carefully
untangled himself and was about to set
off again when he noticed a beautiful
face smiling up at him from the

newspaper. The face of a fairy princess.

Boolar felt his heart flutter. He had never seen a doll so lovely. Carefully, he folded up the paper, put it in his pocket and made his way home. All thoughts of Natty and the Fickles were gone. Now all Boolar could think about was the face in the picture. Where did she come from? Why was she in the newspaper and, most important of all, how could Boolar meet her?

Chapter 7

The betwixt and between time was
coming to an end. The trees were
nearly bare and the leaves had
become playmates for the wind.
Not many legs walked in the
park these days and those that
did left little behind. These were
hard times for the food gatherers.
Sometimes Quilt and Boolar could only
manage to collect half a sack between
them and there seeemed little point in
taking out the pram.

Mr Mouse had made a second
storeroom. He was sure that one would
not be enough to see them through a
long cold winter. It was now ready but
it was empty.

Then one wet and windy afternoon
there was a knock on the front door.
Much to Mr and Mrs Mouse's surprise,
there stood Mr Wolf from the puppet
theatre, umbrella in hand.

Mr and Mrs Mouse took a step
backwards. What could such a grand
and important puppet want with them?

Mr Wolf smiled. 'It is a pleasure to see
you both looking so well,' he said,
with a slight bow.

'Oh, thank you,' said Mrs Mouse, getting all flustered by the honour of Mr Wolf's visit. 'Would you like to come in?'

'Very much, my dear lady, but alas, I am too tall for your charming front door,' said Mr Wolf. 'But if you wouldn't mind taking my umbrella I would be grateful. Now, I have a huge favour to ask you both.'

Quilt, Ting Tang, Boolar, the Countess and Stitch were all in the kitchen wondering what was going on when Mr Mouse called, 'Boolar, come quickly, Mr Wolf wants to speak to you.'

'Me?' said Boolar surprised, but he got up and went down the hall to the front door.

'What do you think is going on?' asked the Countess.

'It must be important,' said Stitch,
'for Mr Wolf to pay us a visit.'

Finally Mr and Mrs Mouse came back
into the kitchen. There was no sign of
Boolar. 'Where's Boolar?' asked Stitch,
running up to them.

'Gone,' said Mrs Mouse, sitting down
at the kitchen table and lifting Stitch
on to her lap.

'Gone where?' said the Countess.

'Gone to the theatre,' said
Mr Mouse grandly.

'When will he be back?'
asked Quilt.

'A day or two at the
most,' said Mr Mouse.

'A day or two at the
most,' they all repeated.

'Why has he gone to the

theatre?' asked Stitch.

'It seems,' said Mr Mouse, 'that a group of travelling puppets is due to open its show tomorrow. They're doing *The Adventures of Tom Thumb*. Unfortunately there has been some sort of mix up and, instead of being sent a leading man, for some reason I can't quite understand, they've been sent a dragon.'

'What's all this got to do with Boolar?' asked the Countess.

'Mr Wolf thought Boolar would make an excellent Tom Thumb,' said Mrs Mouse.

'But he is a doll,' said Ting Tang, 'not a puppet.'

'I know,' said Mr Mouse, a bit flustered. 'But they will fit bracelets to his wrists and ankles so that strings

can be attached and then he will
be a puppet like the others.'

'I suppose they can't do the show
without a Tom Thumb,' said Stitch
thoughtfully.

'But I can't do food gathering without
Boolar,' said Quilt.

'And that is far more important than
being Tom Thumb in a silly puppet
show,' said the Countess firmly.

'Shiver my timbers,' said Quilt.
'How are we going to get the
storeroom filled now?'

'We must remember that Mr Wolf has
done a lot for us,' said Mr Mouse. 'It
was not much to ask and I couldn't very
well say no.'

'Not much to ask!' repeated the
Countess. 'When Boolar is one of the

best food gatherers we have!'

'Well, it's done now,' said Mrs Mouse,
getting up and putting the kettle on the
stove. 'I expect he'll be back in no time.'

Mr Mouse looked sadly around the
second empty storeroom. 'The Countess
is right, my ribbly rodent,' he said.
'It leaves us all in a terrible pickle if
Boolar is gone for more than a day.
Oh, what are we going to do?'

Chapter 8

'Welcome to our humble theatre,' said a very grand puppet, as Mr Wolf brought Boolar up on to the stage.

'This, my dear chap, is the wizard,' said Mr Wolf to Boolar. 'He will be looking after you from now on.'

'I must thank you,' said the wizard, 'for saving us from near disaster.'

Boolar had never seen such a grand puppet before. He was much bigger than Mr Wolf and had blue bushy eyebrows and a flowing gown that glittered.

'I think you should know,' said Boolar shyly to the wizard when Mr Wolf had gone, 'that I am not an actor. I have never ...'

The wizard leant down and whispered

loudly in Boolar's ear. 'You are not to worry. This is a place of magic and wonder where anything is possible.'

He stood up and waved his wand. 'Today a doll,' he said grandly, spreading his arms wide, 'tomorrow a puppet. Now, let me introduce you to your new family of friends and fellow actors. This is Crinkle and this is Crackle.'

Two very heavily made-up lady puppets came over to Boolar. One was as tall as a tower, the other as round as a ball.

'Famed throughout the world,' continued the wizard, 'for playing the Ugly Sisters in *Cinderella*.'

Crinkle put on a pair of small glasses and peered at Boolar down her up-turned nose. 'Charmed, I am sure,' she said in a crinkly voice.

Boolar had just stammered hello when a puff of pink smoke came wafting out from behind a curtain. A dragon in a dressing-gown came lazily up to him and said, 'So you are going to be our Tom Thumb.'

'I ... I don't know,' stuttered Boolar, for the dragon looked as if he could eat Boolar for tea and still have room for biscuits.

'Of course he is, Flake,' said the wizard.

'Remember?'

'Oh yes, I remember,' said Flake. 'I remember that I am the wrong puppet. For the wrong part. Oh, it hurts to think about it,' and he put a scaly claw up to his forehead. 'Why can't I be a star?' A tear rolled down his cheek and he snorted loudly.

Crinkle and Crackle rushed up and put their arms round him.

'We would be lost without you,' said Crackle, handing him a hanky. Flake blew his fiery snout on it, burning a huge hole right through it.

'Oops, sorry,' he said, handing the hanky back to Crackle.

Suddenly a giant butterfly glided down to the stage from above and landed right in front of Boolar. Its painted paper

wings opened and there, to his
amazement, was a fairy princess.

The wizard helped the beautiful tiny
puppet down from the butterfly. 'This,'
he said with pride, 'is Plum, the star of
the show.'

'Oh, how wonderful!' said Boolar. 'I've
seen your picture in the paper.'

Plum looked at Boolar and said in a
voice as sweet as silver bells, 'Yes, he
will do nicely.'

Boolar's heart fluttered for the second time and he fell head over heels in love. He hardly heard what was said next about needing to be cleaned up.

'Crackle,' said Plum. 'Something will have to be done about those rags he is wearing.'

Then in a whoosh of silver dust she disappeared. Boolar stood staring, his mouth wide open, at the spot from which she had vanished.

'Come, come,' said Crackle, taking Boolar's hand.

'Where has she gone?' he asked.

'To get ready for the show,' said Crackle. 'Now let's take you to see your Fairy Godmother.'

'But I don't have a Fairy Godmother. I was left in a box in the park and ...'

mumbled Boolar.

'Take no notice of Crackle, dearie,' said
Crinkle. 'We will take you to see the
puppet master. He can do the necessary.'

Boolar was given a bath. His face
was cleaned and his joints were
made to work like new. Strings
were attached to his wrists and
ankles. Then he was dressed
in a smart little costume
with a waistcoat, a jacket,
a hat and shiny, shiny
shoes. When at last he
caught sight of himself
in the mirror he could
hardly believe his eyes.
The wizard was right.
Even a doll could be
transformed into a puppet.

Chapter 9

Going to the theatre, I am afraid to say, had the same effect on Boolar as the conker had had on Quilt's poor head. He was knocked for six. He found himself in another world full of lights and mirrors where the great outdoors was nothing more than painted scenery and the sun always shone. Here, every evening, a feast was served up on stage under a paper moon.

On the night of the first feast, Boolar was so surprised that he said without thinking, 'Don't you have to go out food gathering?'

Everyone round the table started to laugh.

'What's that when it's at home?' said Flake, blowing a perfect smoke ring up into the air.

'You know, when you go out and collect food that the legs leave behind,' said Boolar a little sheepishly.

'That doesn't sound very nice, dear,' said Crackle.

'Don't tell us that's what you had to do,' said Crinkle.

'Um ... er ... yes,' said Boolar.

'Oh, you poor, poor doll. How awful,' said Plum, putting her tiny hand on his. Boolar's heart beat faster. I didn't choose to be left in that box, he thought, gazing at Plum's beautiful face. But I do choose to be an actor.

Chapter 10

Life in the theatre was so much more
exciting than at Mr and Mrs Mouse's.
For a start, here everything was done
for you. Boolar didn't have to think
about food gathering and none of the
puppets had even heard of betwixt and
between time. As for Jack Frost, they
said he was a puppet who'd been in one
of their shows last year.

'Thank goodness he got lost,' said Flake. 'He was always freezing on stage.'

Crackle giggled.

'What does that mean?' asked Boolar.

'Forgetting his words,' said Flake.

By now *The Adventures of Tom Thumb* had opened. Three times a day Boolar was on stage fighting dragons, rescuing his princess from giants and wizards and living happily ever after. In between performances, he spent most of his time sitting with Plum in her pretty pink dressing room and listening to her stories of life on the open road.

'You should come and travel with us,' said Plum sweetly. 'Oh, I would follow you anywhere,' said Boolar.

Then, the words rushing out so fast
that they tumbled over themselves he
said, 'Will you marry me?'

'Aren't you a sweetheart,' laughed
Plum. She stood up and wrapped a
cloak round her shoulders and put a
crown on her golden curls. 'Now take
my hand and ask me again,
properly this time.'
Boolar knelt down
and kissed her hand.

'Will you marry me?' he said.

'I will,' said Plum.

'But I don't have a ring,' said Boolar.

'Oh, don't worry about that. You can give me one later when you are rich and famous,' said Plum. She took Boolar's hand and sat him down. 'Now that we are going to be married you must tell me all about your life. Where do you come from?' she asked.

Boolar told her about the box and the other dolls and how they had been left, forgotten, under a bush in the park.

'You mean,' said Plum, 'no one came back for you?' A tear rolled down her cheek.

'It was all right,' said Boolar. 'Really. We were saved by Mr and Mrs Mouse who have a ...'

At the word mouse Plum stood up and let out a scream.

'You don't mean real mice with those horrid tails and whiskers?'

'Well …' began Boolar.

'Ugh!' she said. 'I hate mice.'

Then, much to Boolar's shame he said, 'I didn't mean real mice. I meant clockwork mice.'

'Oh,' said Plum, sitting down beside him and taking his hand once more. 'That's quite different. But how could a clockwork mouse save you? I have always found them to be quite useless.'

'Well …' stammered Boolar again.

'You are being shy,' said Plum. 'Oh how enchanting! I bet it was you that saved simply everybody!' She looked at him lovingly and said, 'You are a star.'

Boolar went a little red. 'Sort of,' he mumbled.

At that, Plum leant forward and kissed him on the cheek. 'You're my hero,' she said.

For the rest of the day Boolar felt that he had wings not strings attached to him. He was in love and this was the best day of his life. He was going to join the puppet theatre and see the world and marry his fairy princess.

One thing he vowed never to do again was mention the word mouse.

Chapter 11

The sun always shone on stage and
rain never fell and Boolar soon forgot
all about park life. If he had bothered
to look outside he might have seen his
friends Quilt, the Countess and Mr and
Mrs Mouse out food gathering together.
They were now in terrible danger of
being caught by Mr Cuddles but things
were so bad at home they felt a risk
had to be taken if the storerooms were
ever to be filled.

  The best place by far for food was the
puppet theatre. Here after a show
sweets and cakes and crisps were
dropped. Mr Mouse and Quilt would
rush out in the open, dancing in
between the legs to gather up as much

food as they could.

'Look,' shouted a little boy bending down to do up his shoe laces. 'Daddy, look! A sailor doll!'

Quilt had to run as fast as he could, weaving bravely in between the legs until he reached the safety of the bush where Mr and Mrs Mouse and the Countess were waiting for him.

'Oh twiddle my whiskers, that was too close for comfort,' said Mr Mouse, as Quilt stood gasping for air.

'None of this is right,' said the Countess, looking firmly at the stage door. 'I am going to tell Boolar he must come and help us. That we can't do without him.'

'No, please don't,' said Mr Mouse. 'It's not the way things are done.'

In the park, the flower beds had been dug over and the trees were nearly bare. The betwixt and between time was coming to an end. The days passed into weeks and still Boolar didn't come home.

Life in the box became harder and harder for the dolls. It was becoming chilly and draughty. The wind tickled its way under doors and through cracks until it felt colder inside than it did out.

The Countess had taken to wearing several layers of clothes and two hats.

'And still,' she said miserably, 'I am chilled to the china.'

Then, one very windy morning, the box house began to rattle and shake. The tables and chairs slid this way and that across the floor and the pictures fell off the walls. Nothing seemed very fixed or safe.

'Shiver my timbers,' said Quilt. 'This is like being at sea.'

'You don't think that our little home is going to blow away, do you?' said Ting Tang, holding on to the cupboard.

Before anyone could reply, there was a knock on the front door. The Countess opened it to find Ernst, Mr and Mrs Mouse's nephew, standing there.

'I have just been telling Mr and Mrs Mouse that a horrid howler is on its way to us,' said Ernst.

'What's that when it's at home?' asked Quilt.

'A great storm,' said Ernst, holding on to his hat. 'There's not a minute to lose. I would help if I could but I still have many more families to visit to tell them the news.' And with that he was gone.

Quilt, the Countess and Ting Tang packed up as much as they could and took it to the safety of Mr and Mrs Mouse's house.

'Let's hope Mr Mouse can help us find a way to stop our box blowing away,' said Ting Tang.

Chapter 12

Mr and Mrs Mouse, Quilt and the Countess braved the wind to try to anchor down the box with ropes before it blew away. But the wind was so strong that it took all their strength just to hold the ladder steady.

'Oh twiddle my whiskers,' said Mr Mouse in despair. For every time he managed to get the rope over the box, the wind would lift it up like a piece of string and throw it angrily back at him.

They finally gave up when a gust blew Quilt off his feet and lifted him up into the air like a kite. Luckily the Countess caught him just in time with her umbrella.

'It's no good,' said Mr Mouse. 'We will have to leave it.'

'Leave our lovely home!' said the Countess. 'We can't.'

'What we need is another pair of hands,' said Quilt.

'Maybe if I helped too,' said Ting Tang when they were all safely back in the kitchen, 'we would be able to do it.'

'No,' said Mr Mouse, who was walking backwards and forwards thinking. 'No,' he said again. 'You've been blown away before and the wind wasn't half as strong then. I hate to think what would happen to you this time.'

'If only Boolar was here,' said Mrs Mouse, putting a pan of milk for hot chocolate on the stove.

'That's who we need,' said Stitch. 'Boolar.'

'Oh twiddle my whiskers,' said Mr Mouse, suddenly putting his coat and hat on again.

'Where are you going?' asked the others, astonished.

'To speak to Boolar,' he said. 'It rubs the fur up the wrong way to do it, but I'm sure when he hears that we need him,

he'll come straight home and help.'

'Do be careful my dear,' said Mrs
Mouse. 'Don't you go getting
blown away.'

'Wait,' said Quilt. 'I
want to come with you.'

It took a long time
for the two friends
to reach the theatre.
They had to battle
against the wind all
the way there.

'Now what?' said Quilt
when they finally arrived
wet and bedraggled at
the stage door.

'Oh dear me,' said
Mr Mouse, seeing
a small notice on the

door which read *NO MICE*. 'That's
not really very nice at all!'

'It's horrible,' said Quilt. 'I'll go in and
find Boolar.'

'Well?' said Mr Mouse when Quilt came
out a minute later. 'Did you see him?'

'No,' said Quilt. 'But I saw a puppet
who said he would tell Boolar we are
here. Shouldn't be too long.'

They stood huddled together for what
seemed like ages.

By the time Boolar came out they
were so cold that
they were shivering
and shaking.

'I would ask you in,'
said Boolar, 'but only
actors are allowed
beyond this point.'

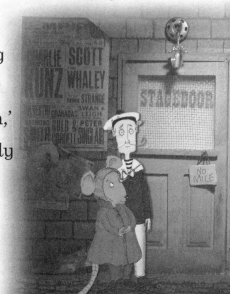

The warmth and light spilling from the stage door looked very inviting and Mr Mouse looked longing at it, nearly forgetting why they were there. 'We've come to tell you,' he said, his teeth chattering, 'that there's a big howler coming tonight.'

'Yes,' said Quilt, 'and we need your help very badly to stop our box from blowing away.'

'Believe me,' added Mr Mouse, 'we wouldn't ask you except this is an emergency.'

Boolar looked down at his shiny, shiny shoes and said, 'Sorry. I can't help tonight. Maybe tomorrow.'

'What!' said Quilt, flabbergasted. 'Can't help your friends! Why not?'

'Because I am the star of *The Adventures of Tom Thumb*,' said Boolar grandly. 'I am a puppet and this is where I live now.'

'My old friend,' pleaded Mr Mouse, 'what are you saying? You are a doll, not a puppet, and this isn't your home.'

'I think I should tell you,' said Boolar stubbornly, 'that you are wrong. I am going to marry Plum and join the theatre for good.'

'Well, shiver my timbers,' said Quilt, amazed as a huge dragon blowing smoke rings from its nostrils came up behind Boolar.

'What have we here? Little friends of yours?' enquired Flake.

'No,' lied Boolar, quickly turning to go back into the theatre. 'No,' he said again. 'They are just lost, that's all. I don't know them, I've never seen them before.'

'I hope not,' said Flake, closing the stage door. 'It would never do

for an actor to
be seen talking
to mice. What
would Plum say?'

Mr Mouse and
Quilt were left
outside in the
dark and the cold.

'I am going to tell Boolar what I think
of him,' said Quilt, jumping up and down
with rage, 'and I am going to bomp that
dragon on the nose.'

'It is no use,' said Mr Mouse, pulling
at Quilt's jacket. 'We will just have
to manage on our own. Come on.'

The two of them made their weary
way back home.

'Where's Boolar?' asked Mrs Mouse
when at last they returned to the house.

'He's not coming,' said Mr Mouse sadly, hanging his soggy coat near the fire to dry. 'He has joined the puppet theatre and he is getting married.'

'No,' said Ting Tang. 'He must come back and help. He wouldn't let us down.'

'The theatre has gone to his head,' said Quilt angrily, wringing the water out of his hat. 'I tell you, he is not the Boolar we all knew and loved. He has changed.'

Mr Mouse went over to the window and looked out at the blackening sky. He could hear the wind singing through the park,

The storm is on its way, the howler's coming out to play.'

Chapter 13

Boolar thought no more about his friends' visit except to hope that Flake hadn't told any of the puppets about him talking to a mouse.

That night, after the show, Boolar went to collect Plum from her dressing room and take her to supper as usual. Except she wasn't there and all the other dressing rooms were empty too.

'Where is everybody?' asked Boolar as he bumped into Mr Wolf backstage.

'Just the chap I want to talk to,' said Mr Wolf, putting a friendly arm round Boolar.

'Have you seen Plum?' Boolar asked.

'It's Plum that I want to speak to you about,' said Mr Wolf. 'Look, old chap, this isn't easy, but the wizard has come to see me. The leading man has turned up. It seems he got lost in left luggage and you're not needed any more. I said I was sure you wouldn't mind as you have a lovely home to go to. Anyway, he ...'

But Boolar wasn't listening. 'Not now,' he said. 'I must find Plum,' and he began walking off towards the stage.

'Wait a minute,' shouted Mr Wolf, 'this is important ...'

On the stage the table was set for supper, the candles were lit and the paper moon was hanging in front of a painted sky.

However, no one was sitting down.

Instead they were all gathered in a little giggling group.

Boolar couldn't see what was going on but he could hear Crackle saying, 'Oh Hero, we have been lost without you.'

'You have no idea how hard it has been having to act with a doll,' said Crinkle.

'What's going on?' asked Boolar.

No one took any notice of him so he said it again, but still no one turned round.

With great difficulty, Boolar pushed his
way to the front to see a sky-blue car
and sitting in it a handsome puppet
with a crown on his head. There next to
him was his Plum.

'What are you doing?' shouted Boolar
rushing forward.

'So this is the doll you have all been
talking about,' said Hero, looking
Boolar up and down.

'As you see, just a poor doll. In no
way a true actor like yourself,'
smarmed the wizard.

'Nice to meet you, I'm sure,' said Hero
looking away, and stroking Plum's
thick golden ringlets. 'Thanks for
helping out, old doll,' he added. 'But
now I am back the real show can begin.'

At this, all the puppets clapped loudly.

'Boolar, bye-bye, that's what I say,' said Hero.

'Isn't he wonderful,' said Flake, 'a true actor,' and he put his scaly claw on his heart. 'One of the best friends a dragon could have.'

'But,' stammered Boolar, 'I thought you didn't like him because you wanted to be the star.'

'Oh,' said the dragon, blowing out a sharp line of fire. 'What would you know about the true nature of an artist like me?'

'Plum,' pleaded Boolar, 'we are going to be married, remember, and live happily ever after.'

'Naughty, naughty,' said Hero,
tickling Plum under the chin.

'I was lonely, my little cockleshell,' she
said, fluttering her long eyelashes at
him. 'It was only make-believe after all.
You're the one I love,' she said, cuddling
up to Hero.

'Make-believe?' said Boolar aghast,
fighting back hot tears. 'Make-believe?
But what about all the plans we had,
the shows we were going to do, the
countries we were going to see?'

Plum got out of the car, helped by
Flake, and stuck her pretty little
nose up in the air.

'You were naughty too,' she said.
'You lied to me, so there. You live with
Mr and Mrs Mouse.'

'I can explain,' said Boolar.

'You told me,' said Flake, 'that you didn't know that mouse and sailor doll. Tut tut! Nasty little liar!'

'Mr Wolf told us all about you and that box you live in,' said Crackle.

'To think,' said Crinkle, 'of our very own Plum having to be seen with mice.'

'Enough,' said Hero. 'You could never marry Plum because, you silly little doll, she is already married to me.'

He put an arm round Plum and said, 'Tomorrow we open with a new show called *The Frog Prince.*'

Boolar felt as if the floor had just fallen away from beneath his feet. He watched, stunned, as Hero took Plum's hand and sat her down at the table.

'We do still need a frog in the show,' said the wizard, taking the last chair. 'Of course it's only a small part but if you are interested, Boolar, it is yours.'

Boolar hadn't moved. Hero looked at Boolar coldly and said, 'This is where the stars eat. Small bit parts like yourself get second sitting.'

Boolar wandered off the stage listening to them laughing.

'Who does he think he is?' said Hero loudly. 'Prince Charming?'

Mr Wolf found Boolar crumpled up in a corner backstage.

'I've lost everything,' said Boolar sadly.

Chapter 14

The howler came to the park like a
terrifying bad-tempered giant banging
on a mighty drum, flashing rods of
lightning. He brought with him his
friend, torrential rain. Together they
ripped up benches and chairs. They tore
up mighty trees by the roots as if they
were toys and hurled them across
paths. They turned puddles into small
rivers that gushed down the gravel
paths and into every crook and cranny.

'It's going to eat us up,' said Stitch
terrified.

'There, there,' said Mrs Mouse,
cuddling him. She couldn't ever
remember a storm as bad as this. The
walls of the house began to shudder and

shake. Pictures and plates, cups and glasses, little ornaments and much-loved tokens came toppling down all around them. Then, just when everyone hoped that the worst was over, there was a terrible groaning and creaking outside. A tree crashed to the ground, shooting its spidery branches in through the window and shattering glass everywhere. At the same moment, the front door gave up its feeble fight against the wind and was blown off its hinges. Now the howler was inside, roaring its way down the hall into the kitchen. It whirled angrily about the little group of friends before blowing open all the storeroom doors. It only left

when a river of rain came rushing into the kitchen flooding the floor.

Mr and Mrs Mouse tried desperately to save Ting Tang and Stitch from getting wet. They all climbed on top of the kitchen table and watched the water rise higher and higher until all the food they had so carefully gathered and cooked bobbed sorrowfully along in the muddy flood.

'Oh dear, oh dear,' wept Mrs Mouse. 'Now what will become of us?'

'There, there, my ribbly rodent,' said Mr Mouse, catching hold of the kettle as it floated past. 'We've been through worse.'

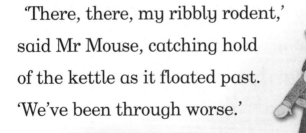

'And worse things happen at sea,'
said Quilt, trying to sound cheerful.

'I can't think what could be worse
than this,' said the Countess, looking
at the soggy mess that had once been
their winter supplies.

The night of the great storm was one
of the longest and most terrible that
any mouse or doll could remember.

The morning light did not shine on
a very merry picture. The flood water had
gone down but Mr and Mrs Mouse's
house was a wreck and nearly all the
food had gone. As for the box house,
it had disappeared altogether under
the fallen tree outside.

Chapter 15

Boolar hadn't heard the storm or if he had, he hadn't taken much notice of it. All he could think of was the storm in his heart.

The following morning he decided to leave the theatre and go to beg Mr and Mrs Mouse to forgive him for being such a fool. He would ask if he could come home.

He set out early before anyone else was awake and was shocked by what he saw. Could this possibly be the same park? It all looked so very different. There were no leaves on the trees and indeed some of the trees had fallen to the ground. Boolar was reminded of a long time ago when he lived in a

playroom and the little girl had thrown
a tantrum, kicking and smashing her
toys. This is what the park looked like
now. He walked back home, avoiding
puddles as wide as ponds. Nothing
looked the same. Had he really been
gone so long?

  When at last he arrived at the bush
where they all lived, he was in for an
even bigger shock, for the box house
was gone, smashed under a fallen tree.
As if that wasn't bad enough, the front
door to Mr and Mrs Mouse's house

had disappeared and pieces of their beloved furniture were all standing higgledy-piggledy outside. The kitchen table was piled high with jars, their neatly-written labels peeling off. Bedclothes and eiderdowns were hanging from washing-lines and everything was dirty, muddy and damp.

'What happened?' cried Boolar as Mr Mouse came round the corner carrying a bucket and mop.

'Boolar,' he said surprised. 'What are you doing here? I thought you were getting married.'

Boolar looked down at his not so shiny, shiny shoes and said, 'I am sorry for the way I behaved.'

'Well, well,' said Mr Mouse kindly, 'don't worry about it.

Nice of you to come and say goodbye.'
He emptied the bucket and went back
into the house. Boolar followed him.

Everyone in the kitchen was busy
trying to save as much as they could.
Ting Tang and Stitch were standing on
chairs so that their feet didn't get wet.
The beautiful little kitchen was in a
terrible mess.

'What can I do to help?' said Boolar,
looking at the cold stove.

'Nothing,' said Quilt crossly.
'You will get your new clothes dirty.'

'I am so sorry,' said Mrs
Mouse coming up to him,
'that we can't offer such a
grand actor as yourself some
tea or cake.' And a tear rolled

down her face.

'There, there, my ribbly rodent, the love of my whiskers, it will be all right. Don't you worry,' said Mr Mouse, putting an arm round her.

'If you have come to ask us to the wedding, we can't attend,' said the Countess stiffly. 'We are too busy.'

'Hope you have a happy life,' said Ting Tang from her chair.

'Yes,' said Mrs Mouse, wiping her eyes on Mr Mouse's hanky. 'Don't let us keep you. Goodbye and good luck.'

'Goodbye,' said Stitch.

Boolar went back outside and walked away, not caring whether Mr Cuddles caught him or not. Never had he felt so bad. What had he done? Why hadn't he gone home and helped when they had asked him to? Now it was all too late. He no longer had a home. All that was left for him was the part of a frog with a company of puppets he never wanted to see again. I deserve to be put on the park keeper's cart and thrown away, he thought to himself miserably. Having nowhere else to go, he trudged back to the theatre, hardly believing that the puppets meant what they had said the night before.

Later that day Mr Wolf found Boolar sitting on a pile of costumes looking very unhappy indeed.

'Come on, old chap, this will never do,' said Mr Wolf.

'I have been so stupid,' said Boolar. 'I let the theatre go to my head, I lied and I let my true friends down.'

Mr Wolf helped Boolar up. 'I think, old fellow, that there's a lot you can do to change things.'

'What?' said Boolar. 'I was ashamed of my friends and I didn't go and help when Mr Mouse asked me to.' Tears rolled down Boolar's face. 'Now their house is ruined and so is ours.'

'Have you eaten?' asked Mr Wolf, taking Boolar into his handsome sitting room. There he sat Boolar in a comfy armchair. He put on the kettle and started toasting muffins over the roaring fire. 'Shall I let you into a secret?' asked Mr Wolf. Boolar nodded his head.

'Plum, Hero, Flake, the wizard, Crinkle and Crackle can't live outside the theatre,' said Mr Wolf. 'Unlike you and me they have strings attached. Their world, if truth were known, isn't as grand as they would have you believe. More often than not it is spent in dark boxes being moved from one theatre to another. And as you know, even the most important puppet can get lost or left behind.'

Mr Wolf handed Boolar a mug of tea and a buttered muffin. Boolar looked at the fire burning merrily in the grate and said miserably, 'I've been so silly, I've lost the best friends a doll could have.'

Just then there was a
loud knock on the door.

'The wizard wants
to know,' said Crackle,
'if that doll there is
going to be a frog. If so, he is wanted
on stage after lunch.' And Crackle
sniffed and closed the door behind her.

'A frog?' said Mr Wolf. 'Is that what
you want to be?'

'No,' said Boolar.

'Hum,' said Mr Wolf. 'Haven't I heard
you talking about a badly-made frog?'

'That's it!' shouted Boolar.
'Thanks for your help, Mr Wolf.'

As he rushed from the theatre
he thought maybe, just maybe,
he could put a wrong right.

Chapter 16

The Fickles had done better in the great storm than Mr and Mrs Mouse on account of the drains that ran all round the boating pond. Apart from the usual drips and leaks, their little home had stood up well to the howler.

Mrs Fickle was very pleased to see Boolar and took him down to the kitchen where a number of little Fickles were happily playing. Natty was sitting on a chair with his feet on the table and a napkin round his neck. As soon as Mrs Fickle came into the room, he complained, 'Not enough. I want sausages.'

'He is like that all day,' said Mrs Fickle shrugging her shoulders. 'He just sits

there wanting food. I tell you, it's giving
Mr Fickle a pain in the tail. We try
to ignore him but it's very hard.'

'Natty,' said Boolar, sitting down at the
table next to him, 'how would you like
to go to a place where the sun always
shines and food never runs out?'

'Oh no, you don't get me like that,
my old doll,' said Natty wearily.
'I am not going out food gathering
with you ever again.'

'No,' said Boolar,
'not food gathering.'

'What then?' said
Natty. 'If you
think you

can winkle me out of here to go and rescue some doll, forget it. My rescuing days are over.'

'The puppets at the theatre are looking for someone to play the part of a frog,' said Boolar. 'There is as much food as you want and everything is done for you. How about that?'

Natty looked suspiciously at Boolar.

'You are not playing silly games, are you?'

'No,' said Boolar, and he started to tell Natty about his time in the theatre. About the meals he had eaten, the clothes he had worn, the snacks he'd been given. You could almost hear a pin drop in the kitchen, for Mrs Fickle and all the little Fickles were listening too, their mouths wide open.

'No food gathering, you're sure?'
asked Natty.

'I'm sure,' said Boolar.

'Let me do it,' interrupted the eldest
of the Fickle children, jumping up and
down excitedly.

'No,' said Natty. 'Only a frog can do this
and you, small tail, are just a rodent.'

Natty got up and, without removing his
napkin, said to a startled Mrs Fickle,
'I don't like living with mice. Never ever
have done and as for your cooking ...'

Boolar quickly put a hand over Natty's mouth before he could say another word and frogmarched him up the hall and out of the front door.

The wizard was waiting for Boolar on the stage, tapping his foot impatiently. Plum stood in the wings bouncing a golden ball up and down.

'Where have you been?' said the wizard angrily when Boolar walked in with Natty.

'Getting you a frog,' said Boolar.

The wizard examined Natty carefully. 'Is that a costume you are wearing?' he asked.

'No, old blue eyebrows, what you see is what you get.

One badly-made frog,' said Natty.

Seeing Plum, he strode over to her.

'Aren't you the sweetest little princess!' said Natty, giving her a kiss.

Plum giggled.

'Natty Bargain, a badly-made frog to your rescue, my little sugar plum.'

'Can you act?' asked Plum smiling.

'For you, yes, as long as there's grub and lots of it,' said Natty.

'Oh,' said Plum. 'What an enchanting frog you are.'

The wizard turned to Boolar.

'I am afraid we don't need you any more, so goodbye.'

Boolar didn't move.

'Haven't you some mouse or other that you should be getting home to?' said the wizard.

'I worked very hard for you and saved your show,' said Boolar. 'In return I would like you to give Mr and Mrs Mouse a gift.'

'You expect us to give a gift to mice!' said the wizard laughing.

'Yes, a gift of food,' said Boolar. 'In fact enough food to fill two storerooms.'

'Food,' said the wizard. 'That's a silly kind of gift. Food is easy-peasy. Everybody has it.'

'Not if you live outside in the park,' said Boolar.

Hero, who had been listening, walked on to the stage swinging a cane. 'We've no intention of giving gifts to thieving mice so you had better be running along,' he said.

'You will never be a proper puppet, because you live with mice,' said Plum haughtily, turning her back on him.

Boolar said, 'Without Mr and Mrs Mouse we dolls would have all been lost in the park. They risked their lives for us which is much more than you would ever do.'

'Ooh la la!' said Hero, 'what a pretty speech. The trouble is that I am pretty sure I'm not cut out for good deeds in the park.'

The others started laughing.

'That's good,' said Natty. 'Pretty sure ...'

Boolar had never remembered feeling so angry as he walked off the stage. He turned and called back to the puppets:

'I can't believe you can be

so ungrateful. Remember, I came here for just one day to help out. Because you needed me, I stayed on when I should have been at home with my friends.'

'Well, go home now,' shouted Hero. 'We're not stopping you. Go home where you belong.'

Suddenly Boolar knew what he was going to do. He ran up the winding staircase to the puppet master's workshop at the top of the theatre where all the puppets' strings were held. He marched noisily over to the puppet master's workbench and picked up the scissors.

Then he leant over and shouted to the puppets below.

'Are you listening to me?' he bellowed. 'Unless you do as I say, unless you give

me food for Mr and Mrs Mouse, I will
cut all your strings now.'

Plum and Hero looked anxiously
at Natty.

'Is he serious?' said Hero.

'I'm just a teeny-weeny little bit scared
of that doll,' lisped Plum.

'We might as well give him some old scraps, don't you think, for his horrid mouse friends,' said Flake.

'I can't understand why any doll would want to live with mice when they could be here,' said Natty. 'I agree with Flake. Let's give him some food and get rid of him.'

'A frog after my own heart,' said Hero laughing.

Chapter 17

An army of mice from all over the park
turned up to help Mr and Mrs Mouse
rebuild their home. Ernst was there with
his pretty wife, Ermintrude, and the
Fickles, as well a large family of mice who
lived by the park gates. They all agreed
that not much could be done about the
dolls' box house. Instead they spent their
time and energy cleaning and scrubbing
for Mr and Mrs Mouse. They laid new
floors and mended windows and doors.
The walls were white washed and soon
the house shone like a new penny.

All the mice waited anxiously as Mr
Mouse carefully opened the hidden door
that led to their winter quarters. They
were worried that they too would be

ruined, and that would be a disaster.
To their great relief the cosy little
sitting room with its fireplace and
armchairs hadn't been damaged at all.

'Oh!' cried the Countess. Her eyes
filled with tears as she looked at the
charming little room. 'It is just like
the Land of Lounge, but better.'

'It's where Mrs Mouse and I spend
the winter months,' explained Mr
Mouse, 'dozing by the fire.'

Ernst repaired the two storerooms. He lined the shelves with paper and what jars could be saved were washed clean and had new labels stuck on them.

After a couple of days' hard work, there were no traces of the terrible damage the howler had brought with it.

There was only one thing that stopped the mice rejoicing. The two storerooms were nearly bare. It was clear to everyone that Mr and Mrs Mouse and the dolls didn't have enough food to make it through the winter.

Now mice are kind and generous in all matters but the stores in the storeroom, the food that has been gathered in the betwixt and between time, is like gold to a mouse. The more he manages to store away, the better his chances of surviving a long hard winter. No mouse worth his whiskers gives away his food at this time of year.

Mr Fickle looked very worried when he said goodbye. He took Mr Mouse's hand and said, 'I am so sorry. And you have been so kind to our family too.'

Mr Mouse looked baffled. 'We have?'

'Yes,' said Mrs Fickle. 'Don't you remember when you sent Boolar over with that sack of food? And yesterday he came back and took Natty away for good.'

'Boolar did that?' said Quilt. 'Well, shiver my timbers.'

'Yes,' said Mr Fickle, 'he did. I will try to send some food to you tomorrow.'

All the other mice said they intended to do the same.

'No,' said Mr Mouse firmly, 'you have all done more than enough in helping us today. None of you must take anything from your storeroom. Mrs Mouse and I won't hear of it, dear friends.'

'I quite agree,' said the Countess.

'We will be fine,' said Ting Tang, shaking each mouse's hand as they filed down the hall and out of the newly-painted front door.

When they had all gone Mrs Mouse put on the kettle for tea. In spite of their worries, its whistle sounded cheerful as they all sat round the kitchen table.

'We could play let's pretend,' said the Countess.

'Good idea,' said Stitch. 'Let's pretend there is a feast in front of us.'

Mr Mouse smiled weakly and stroked his

roly-poly tummy.

Just then the door bell rang.

'It's probably a Fickle who has forgotten something,' said Mr Mouse, wearily making his way up the hall. He opened the door to find Mr Wolf standing there.

'My dear friend,' said Mr Wolf. 'I would like to invite you and your dear wife, the Countess, Quilt, and Ting Tang, not forgetting Stitch of course, to the theatre to see a show and have tea. I think the puppets have something they need to say to you all.'

Chapter 18

Boolar was waiting for them in Mr Wolf's sitting room. A splendid tea had been laid out with a large strawberry sponge cake, biscuits and little sandwiches.

'I am very sorry for the way I behaved,' said Boolar when they were all seated. 'And I wonder if you could forgive me and let me come home.'

Mr Mouse threw his arms round Boolar. 'Of course,' he said. 'Delighted.'

'You mean you don't want to live in the theatre after all?' asked Quilt.

'No,' said Boolar. 'This is not my home.'

The Countess looked at him and said, 'I think you behaved very badly, worse than I could have thought.'

'I know,' said Boolar. 'I was very foolish.'

'Well,' said the Countess stiffly, 'I have to admit that it isn't the same without you.'

'Aren't you getting married then?' asked Stitch.

'No,' said Boolar. 'She had strings attached.'

There was a knock on Mr Wolf's door. Boolar got up to open it. Standing there were the wizard, Crinkle and Crackle,

Flake, Hero and Plum. They all looked
a bit sheepish.

'Come in, all of you,' said Mr Wolf.

Mr and Mrs Mouse stood up. 'Perhaps
we should be getting along.'

'Please stay,' said Mr Wolf. 'I think
Boolar has something he wants to say.'

'First,' Boolar said to the puppets,
'before I leave here, I would like you to
meet some of the kindest and most loyal
friends a doll can have. They have to
battle every day to put food on the table.
They are the most generous
of hosts and they save unwanted dolls
that are left and forgotten.'

'It was nothing,' said Mr Mouse shyly.

'Without them,' continued Boolar, 'we
would all have been torn from limb
to limb by Mr Cuddles, the park

keeper's cat.'

'Hear, hear,' said the Countess, standing up and clapping her china hands.

'Well said,' said Quilt.

Flake was the first of the puppets to come forward. He put his hand on his heart.

'You do all that?' he said. 'I never knew how brave you little things could be.'

Plum and Hero went up to Mr and Mrs Mouse. Plum said, 'I have never met a real mouse before, not to speak to. I do like your shoes,' she said, looking at Mrs Mouse's feet.

'I like yours too,' replied Mrs Mouse.

Hero raised his hand for silence. 'We puppets have been talking amongst ourselves. Boolar very kindly told us all about your misfortune and since we are ...'

Here Hero looked
over at Mr Wolf who
nodded sternly at him.
'... Since we are also most
grateful to Boolar who
came to help us out for
a day but stayed for
so long, we want to
show our gratitude.'
'And to say sorry,'
said Plum,
blowing Boolar
a kiss. 'Are we forgiven?'
'So,' said Crinkle and Crackle together,
'this is our gift from all of us to all of you.'
At that moment the door opened and
ten large hampers were carried in.
Mr Mouse raised the lid of the one
nearest to him and saw hams and

sausages, jars of honey and boxes
of biscuits all packed in straw.

'Oh my! Oh thank you,' said
Mr Mouse, quite overcome.

'But what about you?' said Mrs
Mouse, blowing her nose on a lace-
trimmed hanky. 'How will you manage?'

'Dear lady, our food is brought to us
every day without us having to
lift a finger,' said Hero grandly.

Natty pushed his way into
the room. He looked a little
more squashed than usual but that
didn't stop him from making straight for
the cake. Mr Wolf caught hold of him as
he grabbed the first slice and lifted him
up into the air.

'First things first, Natty,' said Mr Wolf.
'What have you come here to say?'

'One of the hampers is supposed
to be for the Fickles,' said Natty,
'though I think it should go to me.'

'If you say another word, my badly-
made friend, no more cake for you,' said
Mr Wolf, and everyone started to laugh.

The tea party was a great success.
Dolls, puppets and mice found they
had more things in common than
they expected. If it hadn't been for
the fact that the puppets were
needed on stage to perform *The Frog
Prince* the party would have gone on
well into the night.

'Who would have thought the puppets
could be so kind hearted,' said Mr Mouse
when they had gone to start the show.

'That's the trouble really,' said Mr Wolf.
'You see, their hearts are mostly made of

mirrors so they spend a lot of time thinking about themselves. They think they are more important than they really are. Then someone like Boolar comes along and reminds them how lost they would be without strings.'

'All the same,' said Quilt to Mr Wolf as he helped them carry the hampers home, 'We would have been lost without their kindness.'

'You have Boolar to thank for that,' said Mr Wolf.

Along the way they stopped off at the

Fickles' house. Mr Fickle looked worried when he opened the front door but could hardly believe his good fortune when Boolar explained that the hamper of food was a gift from Natty.

By the time the little group of friends had reached Mr and Mrs Mouse's front door, a fingernail moon shone in the sky. They said goodnight to Mr Wolf and let themselves into the snug little house.

If you looked through Mr and Mrs Mouse's kitchen window that evening, you would have seen a very happy sight indeed. A table laid for a fine dinner and

five dolls and two mice, all happy
to be together again.

Mr Mouse stood and raised his glass.

'To friends!' he said.

The dolls all stood up and raised
their glasses.

'To friends!' repeated Boolar, looking
round the room. He sat down again,
contented. Now he knew for certain
where his home was and where

his heart belonged.